Using this book

When going through this book
with your child, you can either read through
the story first, talking about it
and discussing the pictures,
or start with the sounds pages
at the beginning.

If you start at the front of the book,
read the words and point to the pictures.
Emphasise the **sound** of the letter.

Encourage your child to think
of the other words beginning with
and including the same sound.
The story gives you the opportunity
to point out these sounds.

After the story, slowly go through the
sounds pages at the end.

Always praise and encourage
as you go along. Keep your
reading sessions short and stop
if your child loses interest.

Throughout the series, the order in which the sounds
are introduced has been carefully planned to
help the important link between reading and writing.
This link has proved to be a powerful boost to
the development of both skills.

SOUNDS FEATURED IN THIS BOOK

a   d   g   qu   ai   au   aw
ar   ay   dr   gr

The sounds introduced are repeated
and given emphasis in the practice books,
where the link between reading and writing is at the
root of the activities and games.

Ladybird books are widely available, but in case of
difficulty may be ordered by post or telephone from:

Ladybird Books – Cash Sales Department
Littlegate Road Paignton Devon TQ3 3BE
Telephone 0803 554761

A catalogue record for this book is available
from the British Library

Published by Ladybird Books Ltd Loughborough Leicestershire UK
Ladybird Books Inc Auburn Maine 04210 USA

Text copyright © Jill Corby 1993
© LADYBIRD BOOKS LTD 1993

Say the Sounds
The
go-cart race

by JILL CORBY
illustrated by RAY MUTIMER

Aa

apple

ant

acrobat

alligator

Read the words. Say the sound.

and   as   at   am

add   atlas   anger

pan   man   fan

 arrow

 antler

Dd

Say the sound.

dog

dark

doughnut

day

did

door

dam

does

don't

deep

dad

ditch

dig

Gg

Say the sound.

give

gate

got

go

goat

get

good

game

gas

garage

gave

Qu qu

q is never without a u and usually sounds like kw

Quiff

queen

quite

queue

quick   quiet

quins

quack!

quack

quilt

Aunt Ann has a tree.

Ben likes to climb the tree.

Jenny climbs high in the tree. Next Aunt Ann climbs high in the tree.

Jenny is high in the tree.
She sees a blue go-cart.

"Can you see the go-cart,
Ben?" she asks. "I like the
go-cart," she says.

"Can we make a go-cart please, Dad?" Ben asks.

"Come on, Jenny. We must look for some wood," says Ben.

Jenny finds some wood. "Dad, come here and look. Here is some wood," she says.

Now they can make a
go-cart.

"Can we make it here?"
Ben asks.

Aunt Ann finds some nails.
Dad finds some hammers.

Aunt Ann hammers in some nails. Jenny and Ben hammer in some nails.

"Look where Quiff is now,"
says Ben to Jenny.
"He can't jump on here,"
Ben says.

"No, Quiff. You can't jump now," Ben says.

"Please jump here, Quiff," says Jenny.

"Look, Ben. I can see a crocodile in a go-cart," says Jenny. "Can we pass him?"

No, they can't pass the crocodile here.

"Come on. We can pass his
go-cart now," says Ben.

Then they see the frog in his go-cart.
He is going very fast.

"Can we go very fast and pass him?" Jenny asks.

Can they pass him?

Yes, they can!

Imp's go-cart is going faster
and faster.
Jenny and Ben go faster,
too.

They can't pass Imp.

Now they can pass Imp.
He was going too fast!

Next they have to pass
Octopus in his red go-cart.
They have to go very fast.

They have to pass Troll next. He is going faster and faster.

Jenny and Ben go faster, too. Then they pass him.

Now they can see Snake.
He has a blue go-cart.

Snake is going very fast.
"You can't pass here,"
he shouts.

Ben and Jenny see his blue
go-cart. It is high in the
tree.
He was going too fast.

Then Ben and Jenny
pass him.

"I can see Quiff now," Ben says. "Dad, we have won!" he shouts.

"Aunt Ann, we have won!" shouts Jenny.
"We have won!" they shout.

ai

Say the sound.

sail

mail

tail

paint

hail

nail

au

caught

astronaut

taught

aw sounds the same

dawn

lawn   fawn

ar

dark

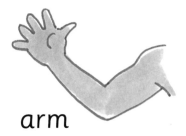

arm

farm

hard

dart

card

armour

alarm

part

start

cart

tarts

ay

Say the sound.

say

hay

day

rays

may

play

way

stay

away

bay

clay

lay

jay

pay

dr

Say the sound.

dragon

dream

dress

drain

drink

drive

drip

drum

drop

gr

Say the sound.

green

granny

grandma

great

grow

grin

grey

greet

grunt

growl

grip

grass

Match the sound to the correct picture.

g

au

dr

New words used in the story

Words introduced 36

Learn to read with Ladybird

Read with me

A scheme of 16 graded books which uses a look-say approach to introduce beginner readers to the first 300 most frequently used words in the English language (Key Words). Children learn whole words and, with practice and repetition, build up a reading vocabulary.

Support material: Pre-reader, Practice and Play Books, Book and Cassette Packs, Picture Dictionary, Picture Word Cards

Say the Sounds

A phonically based, graded reading scheme of 8 titles. It teaches children the sounds of individual letters and letter combinations, enabling them to feel confident in approaching Key Words.

Support material:
Practice Books, Double Cassette Pack, Flash Cards

Read it yourself

A graded series of 24 books to help children to learn new words in the context of a familiar story. These readers follow on from the pre-reading series, **Read together**, and can be used in conjunction with any Ladybird reading scheme.